SNIFF! SNIFF!

BY
RYAN SIAS

Abrams Appleseed
New York

Library of Congress Cataloging-in-Publication Data

Sias, Ryan, author, illustrator.
Sniff! sniff! / by Ryan Sias.
pages cm
Summary: Illustrations and minimal text reveal the thoughts of an energetic puppy as he busily sniffs his
way in and around the house, and the reader can guess where the pup will be going when the page is turned.
ISBN 978-1-4197-1490-0
[1. Dogs—Fiction. 2. Animals—Infancy—Fiction. 3. Smell—Fiction.] I. Title.
PZ7.S56265Sni 2015
[E]—dc23
2014016111

Text and illustrations copyright © 2015 Ryan Sias
Book design by Meagan Bennett

Printed and bound in China
10 9 8 7 6 5 4 3 2 1

For bulk discount inquiries, contact specialsales@abramsbooks.com.

ABRAMS
THE ART OF BOOKS SINCE 1949
115 West 18th Street
New York, NY 10011
www.abramsbooks.com

Dedicated to
ABBY and SIMON,
whose love cured
my fear of dogs

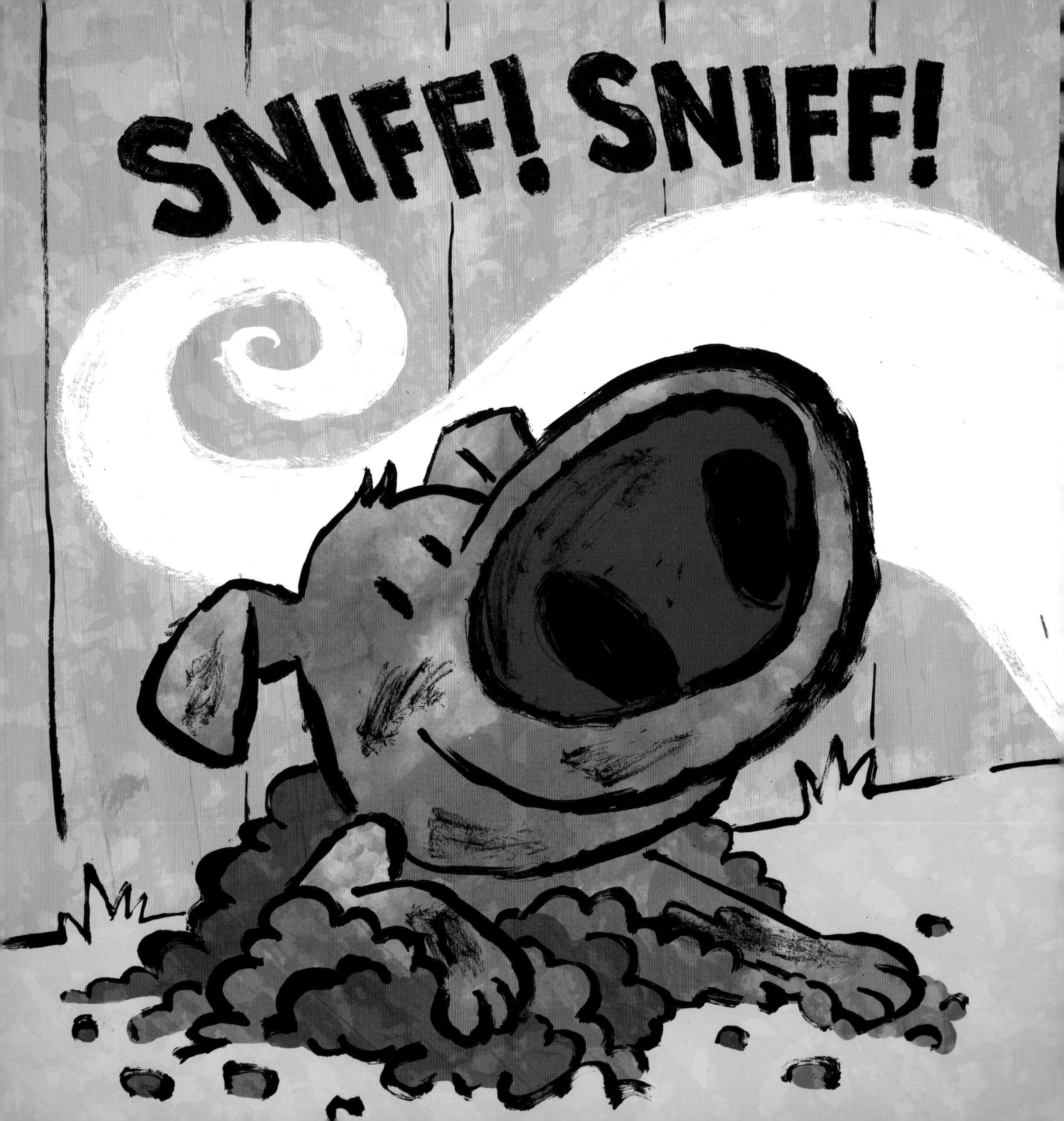
SNIFF! SNIFF!

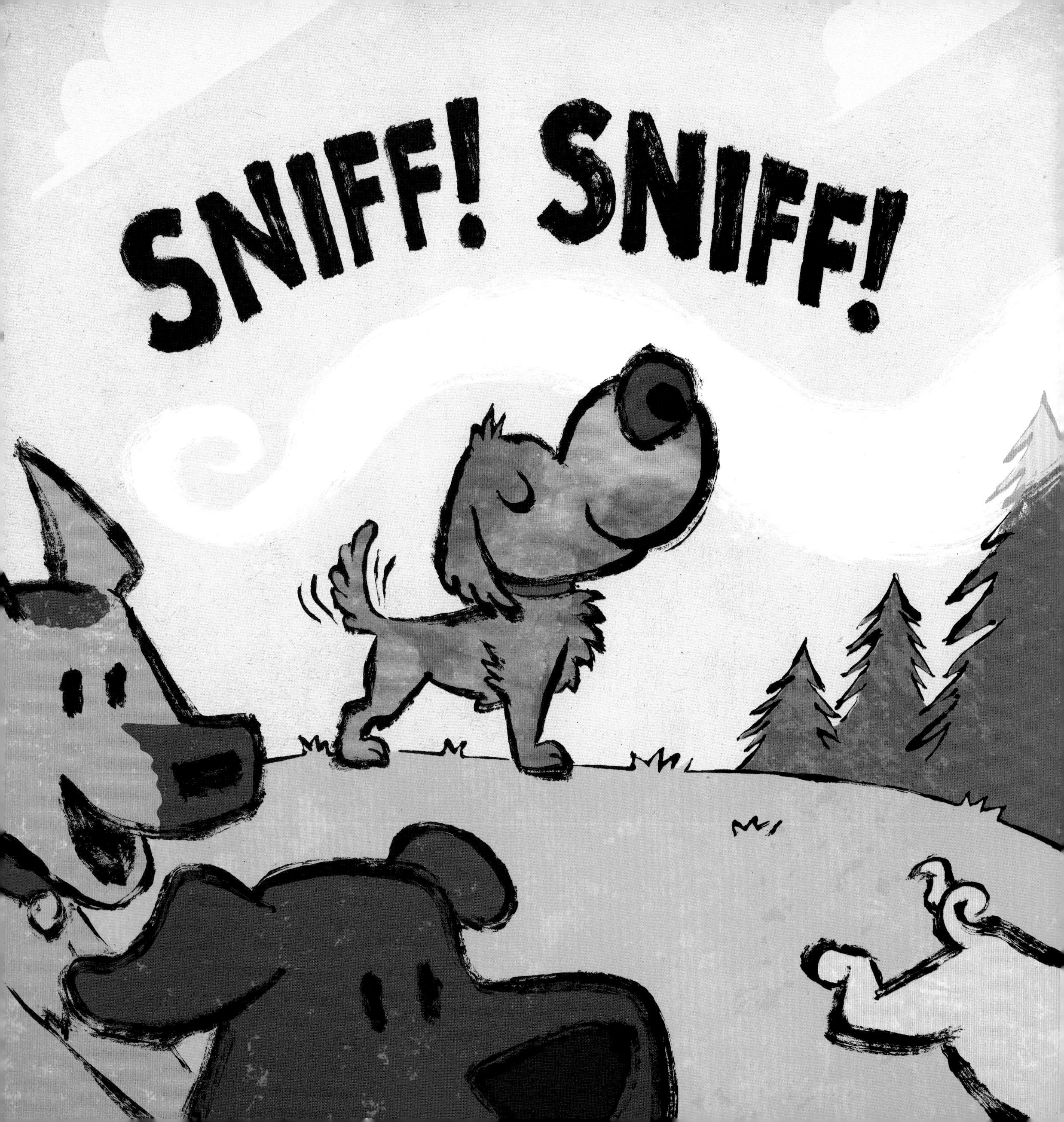
SNIFF! SNIFF!